Community Soup

Alma Fullerton

pajamapress

For my mother; and for Grandpa Talbot, who taught me that gardening can provide nourishment for both body and soul.

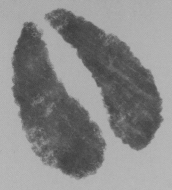

First published in the United States in 2013
Text and illustrations copyright © Alma Fullerton
This edition copyright © 2013 Pajama Press

10 9 8 7 6 5 4 3 2 1

Canada Council   Conseil des arts
for the Arts   du Canada

ONTARIO ARTS COUNCIL
CONSEIL DES ARTS DE L'ONTARIO

The publisher gratefully acknowledges the support of the Canada Council for the Arts and the Ontario Arts Council for its publishing program. We acknowledge the financial support of the Government of Canada through the Canada Book Fund (CBF) for our publishing activities.

Library and Archives Canada Cataloguing in Publication

Fullerton, Alma
    Community soup / Alma Fullerton.
ISBN 978-1-927485-27-9
    I. Title.
PS8611.U45C64 2013   jC813'.6   C2012-906891-8

Publisher Cataloging-in-Publication Data (U.S.)

Fullerton, Alma, 1969-
    Community soup / Alma Fullerton.
[32] p. : col. ill. ;   cm.
Summary: In a garden outside a Kenyan schoolhouse, the children work together to harvest the vegetables they have grown and make them into a soup for everyone to share, but Kioni's goats have followed her to school today and they are trying to eat all the vegetables.
ISBN-13: 978-1-927485-27-9
1. Community gardens – Kenya – Juvenile fiction. 2. Community kitchens – Kenya – Juvenile fiction. 3. Kenya – Social life and customs – Juvenile fiction. I. Title.
[E] dc23   PZ7.F855Co 2013

Manufactured by Sheck Wah Tong Printing Ltd.
Printed in Hong Kong, China.

Pajama Press Inc.
469 Richmond St E, Toronto Ontario, Canada
www.pajamapress.ca

Distributed in the U.S. by **Orca Book Publishers**
PO Box 468 Custer, WA, 98240-0468, USA

It's soup day!
Outside the schoolhouse,
the teachers stir the broth.

But where are the vegetables?

In the community garden,
Jomo picks a pumpkin.
Dalila plucks some beans.

But where is Kioni?

Kioni is late. She still has chores
to do at home. She rushes to feed her—

"OH! But where are the goats?"

In the garden,
Matu digs sweet potatoes.
Amundi bundles corn.

But where is Kioni? She is
looking for her—

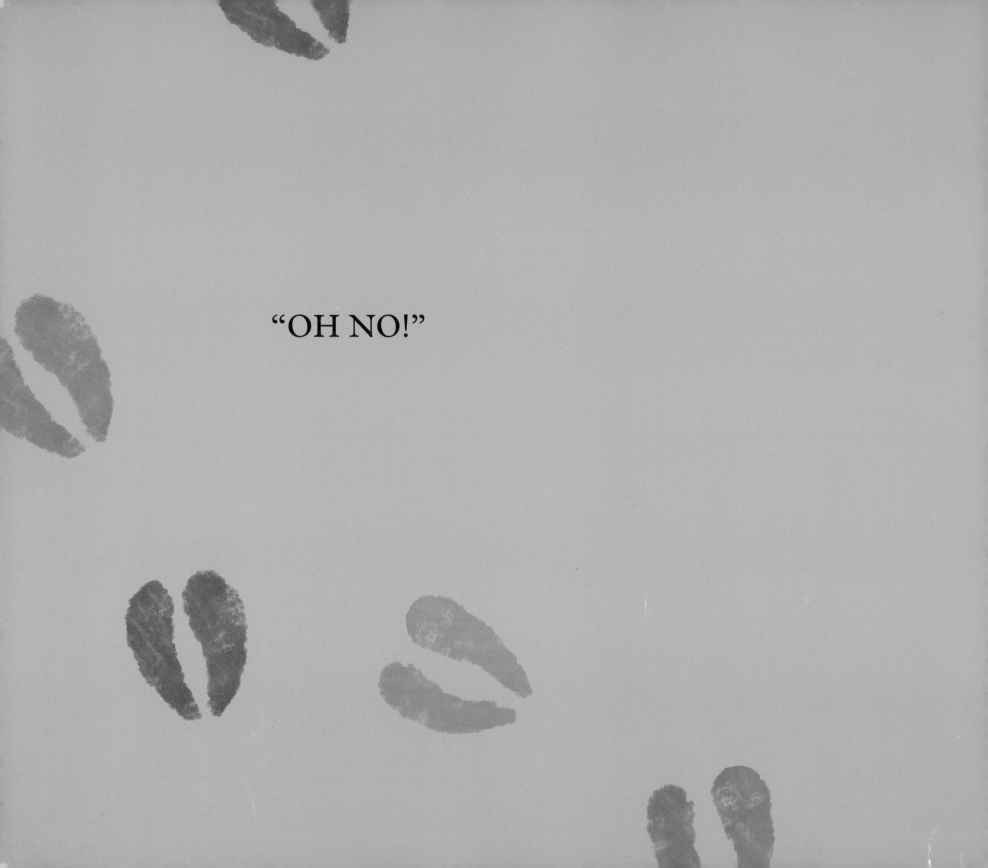

"OH NO!"

Kioni has a herd of goats,
with hair of calico.

And everywhere Kioni goes,
those goats are sure to—

They trotted off to school today,
which breaks the No Goats rule.

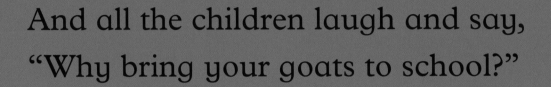

And all the children laugh and say,
"Why bring your goats to school?"

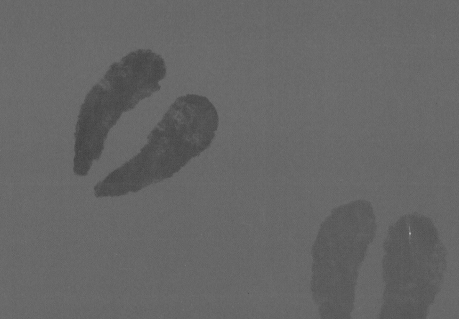

"Those pesky goats make me so mad.
It's as if they're never fed.
I'd like to put them in the soup—"

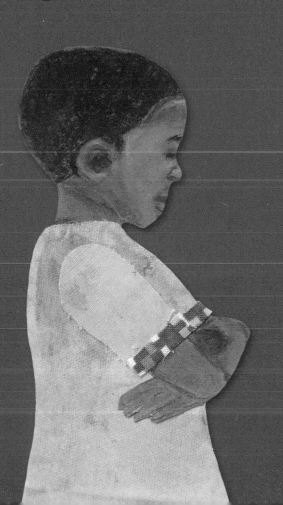

"NO!

"We can add their milk instead!"

Pumpkin Vegetable Soup

(with help from an adult)

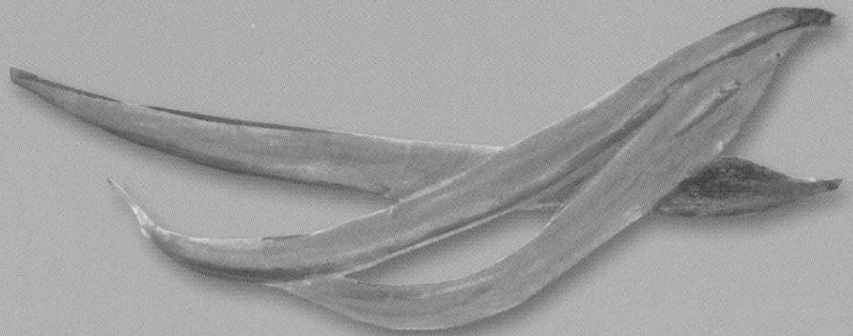

Peel and chop:
1 cup of **pumpkin**
1 **sweet potato**
1 cup of mixed **vegetables** (**beans**, **carrots**, **corn**, **celery**)
1 large **onion**

Put everything in a large soup pot and add:
6 cups of **vegetable stock**
1 inch of **gingerroot**, peeled and minced
1 stick of **cinnamon** .

Bring the pot to a boil, then reduce it to a simmer and add:
2 cloves of **garlic**, chopped
1/4 teaspoon each of **parsley**, **basil**, and **chili flakes**
(leave out the chili if you want)

Simmer for about 30 minutes, then add:
1/2 cup of **goat's milk** (you can use regular milk or coconut milk)
salt and **pepper** (not too much!)

Turn off the heat and take out the **cinnamon** stick.
Use a hand blender to puree the soup.
Serve the soup with diced **red pepper** and **parsley** sprinkled on top. Enjoy!